SYLVIA PLATH

A Dramatic Portrait

SYLVIA PLATH

A DRAMATIC PORTRAIT

conceived and adapted from her writing

by

BARRY KYLE

FABER AND FABER LTD

3 Queen Square

London

58483

First published in 1976
by Faber and Faber Limited
3 Queen Square, London W C 1
Reprinted 1977
Printed and bound in Great Britain by
Whitstable Litho Ltd, Whitstable, Kent
All rights reserved

ISBN 0 571 10698 6

SYLVIA PLATH: A DRAMATIC PORTRAIT was first
presented by the Royal Shakespeare Company in
October 1973 at The Place under the direction of Barry
Kyle. The cast was as follows:

Sylvia 1	Louise Jameson
Sylvia 2	Brenda Bruce
Sylvia 3	Estelle Kohler

Acknowledgements are due to Weidenfeld and Nicolson
for permission to quote from THE SAVAGE GOD by
A. Alvarez and to the editors of THE NEW STATESMAN
and THE LONDON MAGAZINE for permission to quote
from these journals.

NOTE

The text of this 'dramatized setting' was compiled as a
companion piece to <u>Three Women</u>, Sylvia Plath's play
about childbirth.

In <u>Three Women</u> there is a constantly shifting
perspective as the three separate accounts of childbirth
merge and contrast. Similarly, this script is based on
the device of three Voices; each playing Sylvia Plath at
different times. It was compiled very much with the
R. S. C. cast in mind, and any group tackling this script
should feel free to re-organise the sharing-out of the
material according to its own character.

There are no entrances and exits in the play. In the
R. S. C. production the cast was used like a chorus to
back-up the situation of each poem; or they sat simply on
the floor when not speaking, and listened. They wore
identical costumes. The setting was a surround of
stretched white gauze and white carpet, with a blow-up
photograph of Sylvia Plath in one corner. There was no
furniture, but many simple naturalistic props were used
to identify the changes of situation.

To keep traces of a plain, story-telling style the
action was punctuated by the silent changing of caption-
cards which introduced phases of action ('Country Life',
'Primrose Hill' etc.). Some bits of narrative we chose

9

to read, rather than learn, for the same stylistic reason.

Finally, a word about the poems. Most of them were spoken directly to the audience, as if the audience were the pages of a diary. The objectivity of tone this created was most important. Clearly, the whole programme rests on the fact that most of the poems have an actable dramatic situation at their root. So, for instance, Estelle Kohler peeled a saucepanful of potatoes during her extract from 'Lesbos'; 'Daddy' was played as an exorcism in nursery rhyme while kneeling round a swastika.

The poems prove, I think, to be marvellous theatre - provided the theatre interprets them without emotional wallowing, or flat poetic reciting.

BARRY KYLE

SYLVIA PLATH

SETTING: A chamber of draped white gauze with a large,
    photographic portrait of Sylvia Plath. Behind the
    gauze, at the back of the set, there hangs a trans-
    lucent moulding of the Death-Mask of Blake.
    Spotlight. A still figure.

FIGURE: Colour floods to the spot, dull purple.
             The rest of the body is all washed out,
             The colour of pearl.

             In a pit of rock
             The sea sucks obsessively,
             One hollow the whole sea's pivot

             The size of a fly,
             The doom mark
             Crawls down the wall.

             The heart shuts,
             The sea slides back,
             The mirrors are sheeted.   ('Contusion')

VOICE (from The Savage God by A. Alvarez): Out of her
    death a whole myth has grown. It is a myth of the

poet as a sacrificial victim, offering herself up for the sake of her art. In these terms, her suicide becomes the whole point of the story, the act which validates her poems, gives them their interest and proves her seriousness. Yet just as the suicide adds nothing at all to the poetry, so the myth of Sylvia as a passive victim is a total perversion of the woman she was. It misses altogether her liveliness, and harsh wit, her vehemence of feeling, her control. Above all, it misses the courage with which she was able to turn disaster into art. The pity is not that there is a myth of Sylvia Plath but that the myth is not simply that of an enormously gifted poet whose death came carelessly and too soon.

(A baby cries.)

VOICE: What is so real as the cry of a child?
     The clear vowels rise like balloons.

VOICE: On October 27th 1932 Sylvia Plath was born at Robinson Memorial Hospital in Boston, Massachusetts. Her parents chose her name for its association with the herb 'Salvia' and the poetic adjective 'sylvan'.

VOICE: Her mother, Aurelia Schober, was a Boston woman of Austrian parents. She met her husband while studying for a Master's degree in German, at Boston University.

VOICE: Her father, Otto Plath, came to the United States at fifteen from a small town in the Polish corridor. He was Professor of Biology at Boston University, distinguished in ornithology, entomology, and ichthyology, and the well-known author of a treatise on bees 'Bumblebees and their ways'. At her birth Otto Plath announced:

12

OTTO: All I want from life from now on is a son born
two and a half years to the day.

VOICE: Mrs. Plath obligingly brought forth Warren
Joseph on April 27th 1935. Exactly two and a half
years to the day. Professor Plath's colleagues
toasted him as

ALL (toasting): The man who gets what he wants when he
wants it.

(Distant sounds of the sea.)

SYLVIA 3: My childhood landscape was not land but the
end of the land - the cold, salt, running hills of the
Atlantic.

(Enter young SYLVIA with a bucket containing seawater and seashells. She sits with the bucket
between her knees and examines the shells.)

I collected shells. The shells of blue mussels with
their rainbowy angel's fingernail interior and purple
'lucky stones' with the white ring all the way round.

SYLVIA 1: You can always tell where the best shells are -
at the rim of the last wave, marked by a mascara of
tar.

SYLVIA 3: I sometimes think my vision of the sea is the
clearest thing I own.

(Young SYLVIA starts to spread out shells on the
floor.)

SYLVIA 3: All this was before the birth of my brother.
Then one day the textures of the beach burned themselves on the lens of my eye forever. Hot April. I
warmed my bottom on the mica-bright stone of my
grandmother's steps. My mother was in hospital.
She had been gone three weeks. I sulked. I would do
nothing. Her desertion punched a smouldering hole
in my sky. How could she, so loving and faithful,

13

leave me? My grandmother hummed and thumped
out her bread dough with suppressed excitement.
Viennese, Victorian, she pursed her lips, she would
tell me nothing. Finally she relented a little. I
would have a surprise when Mother came back. It
would be something nice. It would be - a baby.

SYLVIA 1 (appalled): A baby!

SYLVIA 3: I hated babies. Hugging my grudge I trudged
off on my own. As from a star I saw the separ-
ateness of everything. I felt the wall of my skin: I am
I. That stone is a stone.

(She has picked up one of young SYLVIA's shells.)

SYLVIA 1 (to audience): Sometimes I nursed starfish
alive in jam-jars of seawater and watched them
grow back lost arms. On this day, this awful birth-
day of otherness, my rival, somebody else, I flung
the starfish against a stone.

SYLVIA 3: My beautiful fusion with the things of this
world was over. I recall my mother, a sea-girl
herself, reading to me and my brother from
Matthew Arnold's 'Forsaken Merman'.

MOTHER: Sand-strewn caverns, cool and deep,
        Where the winds are all asleep;
        Where the spent lights quiver and gleam;
        Where the salt-weed sways in the stream;
        Where the sea-beasts ranged all round
        Feed in the ooze of their pasture-ground;
        Where the sea-snakes coil and twine
        Dry their mail and bask in the brine;
        Where great whales come sailing by,
        Sail and sail with unshut eye,
        Round the world forever and aye.

SYLVIA 1 (turns to audience): I saw the gooseflesh on my

skin. I did not know what made it. I was not cold.
Had a ghost passed over?

SYLVIA 3: No, it was the poetry. A spark flew off Arnold
and shook me, like a chill.

SYLVIA 1: I wanted to cry; I felt very odd.

SYLVIA 3: I had fallen into a new way of being happy.

VOICE: She began to hide little poems in her
mother's dinner napkin or beneath the
butter plate.

SYLVIA 1: Liver, liver.

Makes me shiver.

VOICE: At eight and a half she wrote to the <u>Boston Sunday
Herald</u>.

SYLVIA 1: Dear Editor: I have written a poem about what
I see and hear on hot summer nights.

Hear the crickets chirping
In the dewy grass.
Bright little fireflies
Twinkle as they pass.

Thank you for my Good Sport pin. Sylvia Plath (age
$8\frac{1}{2}$ years).

SYLVIA 3: On November 2nd 1940, following a long and
difficult illness, Otto Plath died.

(The mask of Blake is slowly illuminated.)

SYLVIA 1: I thought that if my father hadn't died he would
have taught me all about insects which was his
speciality at the University. He would also have
taught me German and Greek and Latin. My mother
hadn't let us go to the funeral, because we were only
children, and he had died in hospital, so the grave-
yard and even his death had always seemed unreal to
me.

VOICE: At the age of thirty-two she wrote a poem about a

15

girl whose father died while she thought he was God. The father is imagined as a Nazi and the mother as very possibly part Jewish, in the daughter the two strains marry and paralyse each other.

(They open out a swastika.)

SYLVIA 1: Daddy.

SYLVIA 3: You do not do, you do not do
> Any more, black shoe
> In which I have lived like a foot
> For thirty years, poor and white,
> Barely daring to breathe or Achoo.
> Daddy, I have had to kill you.

SYLVIA 1: You died before I had time -
> Marble-heavy, a bag full of God,
> Ghastly statue with one grey toe
> Big as a Frisco seal
> And a head in the freakish Atlantic
> Where it pours bean green over blue
> In the waters off beautiful Nauset.

SYLVIA 2; I used to pray to recover you.
> Ach, du.
> In the German tongue, in the Polish town
> Scraped flat by the roller

SYLVIA 1, 2, 3:
> Of wars, wars, wars.

SYLVIA 3: But the name of the town is common.
> My Polack friend
> Says there are a dozen or two.
> So I never could tell where you
> Put your foot, your root,
> I never could talk to you.
> The tongue stuck in my jaw.
> It stuck in a barb wire snare.

                    Ich, ich, ich, ich,

SYLVIA 1: I could hardly speak.

          I thought every German was you.

SYLVIA 2: And the language obscene

SYLVIA 1, 2, 3:

          An engine, an engine

SYLVIA 2: Chuffing me off like a Jew.

          A Jew to Dachau, Auschwitz, Belsen.

          I began to talk like a Jew.

SYLVIA 3: I think I may well be a Jew.

SYLVIA 1: The snows of the Tyrol, the clear beer of

              Vienna

          Are not very pure or true.

          With my gipsy ancestress and my weird luck

SYLVIA 3: And my Taroc pack and my Taroc pack

SYLVIA 1: I may be a bit of a Jew.

SYLVIA 2: I have always been scared of you,

          With your Luftwaffe, your gobbledygoo.

SYLVIA 1: And your neat moustache

SYLVIA 3: And your Aryan eye, bright blue.

SYLVIA 2: Panzer-man, panzer-man, O You—

          Not God but a swastika

          So black no sky could squeak through.

SYLVIA 3: Every woman adores a Fascist,

          The boot in the face, the brute

          Brute heart of a brute like you.

SYLVIA 1: You stand at the blackboard, daddy,

          In the picture I have of you,

          A cleft in your chin instead of your foot

          But no less a devil for that, no not

          Any less the black man who

          Bit my pretty red heart in two.

          I was ten when they buried you.

                                                    17

At twenty I tried to die
And get back, back, back to you.
I thought even the bones would do.
But they pulled me out of the sack,
And they stuck me together with glue.
And then I knew what to do.

SYLVIA 3: I made a model of you,
A man in black with a Meinkampf look
And a love of the rack and the screw.
And I said I do, I do.
So daddy, I'm finally through.
The black telephone's off at the root,
The voices just can't worm through.
If I've killed one man, I've killed two —
The vampire who said he was you
And drank my blood for a year,
Seven years, if you want to know.
Daddy, you can lie back now.
There's a stake in your fat black heart
And the villagers never liked you.
They are dancing and stamping on you.
They always <u>knew</u> it was you.
Daddy, daddy, you bastard, I'm through.

('Daddy')

(Sounds of the sea - the Death-Mask fades.)

VOICE: Otto Plath's death changed Sylvia's life radically
within a few months. Her mother decided to live
inland, thinking that Sylvia's acute sinusitis might
benefit from a drier climate. From that point Sylvia
Plath felt a constant longing for the sea.

SYLVIA 3: My final memory of the sea is of violence - a
still, unhealthily yellow day in 1939, the sea molten,
steely-slick, heaving at its leash like a broody

animal, evil violets in its eye.

(The sea fades.)

VOICE: The Plath family now lived in Wellesley; Sylvia
went to the Marshall Livingston Perrin Grammar
School, and then the Gamaliel Bradford Senior High
School. She started art lessons and sketches began
to appear beneath the butter plate. With her first
sample of artwork she won 1 dollar in a newspaper
contest.

(SYLVIA 1 moves to centre, sketching.)

SYLVIA 3: I went to public schools - genuinely public.
Everybody went: the podge, the gangler, the future
cop who would one night kick a diabetic to death
under the mistaken impression he was a drunk and
needed cooling off; the poor, smelling of sour wools
and the urinous baby at home; the richer, with ratty fur
collars and daddies with cars.

VOICE: Wot does your daddy do?

VOICE: He don't woik, he's a bus droiver.

SYLVIA 3: There it was - Education - laid on free of
charge for the lot of us. Every morning, hands on
hearts, we pledged allegiance to the Stars and Stripes,
a sort of aerial altarcloth over teacher's desk. And
sang songs full of powder-smoke and patriotics to
wobbly soprano tunes.

VOICE (as teacher announcing the hymn): 'For purple
mountain majesties above the fruited plain.'

SYLVIA 3: In those days I couldn't have told a fruited
plain from a mountain majesty! But the hymn always
made the scampi-sized poet in me weep, so I warbled
nevertheless, with my small snotty compatriots . . .

ALL (singing): 'America, America! God shed his grace
on thee and crown thy good with brotherhood from

19

sea to shining sea.'

SYLVIA 3: I mostly remember myself as a gawky mess with drab hair and bad skin.

VOICE: She was co-editor of her school newspaper The Bradford.

SYLVIA 3: Was on the girls' basketball team.

VOICE: She painted decorations for class dances.

SYLVIA 3: Was Lady Agatha in the class play The Admirable Crichton.

VOICE: And was described in her High School yearbook, the Wellesleyan:

SYLVIA 1: 'Warm smile . . . energetic worker . . . Bumble Boogie piano special . . . clever with chalk and paints . . . future writer.' Gawky mess?
(They re-assemble. SYLVIA 1 hands SYLVIA 2 a large red leather thesaurus.)

SYLVIA 3: The blood jet is poetry
There is no stopping it.
(SYLVIA 2 sits with thesaurus and papers, writing.)

VOICE: In September 1950 Sylvia Plath entered Smith College on a scholarship and began to write poetry on a precise schedule. She sat with her back to whoever entered the room and circled words in the red leather Thesaurus which had belonged to Otto Pla~ After suffering through blind date after blind date on successive weekends of her first semester, she deci~ to stay in on Saturday nights and talk with a friend or go to bed early.

VOICE: From Sylvia Plath's novel The Bell Jar : Esther Greenwood at college.
(SYLVIA 1 puts on baseball cap.)

SYLVIA 2: I saw a lot of Buddy Willard. He was two years older than I was and very scientific. Suddenly, after

20

I finished a poem, he said -

BUDDY: Esther, have you ever seen a man?

SYLVIA 2: The way he said it I knew he didn't mean a man in general. I knew he meant a man naked. No, only statues.

BUDDY: Well, don't you think you would like to see me?

SYLVIA 2: I didn't know what to say. All I'd heard about was how fine and clean Buddy was, and how he was the kind of person a girl should stay fine and clean for. So I didn't really see the harm in anything Buddy would think up to do. (to BUDDY) Well all right I guess so. I stared at Buddy while he unzipped his chino pants and took them off and then took off his underpants that were made out of something like nylon fishnet.

BUDDY: They're cool and my mother says they wash very easily.

SYLVIA 2: All I could think of was turkey neck and turkey gizzards. I felt very depressed.

BUDDY: I think you ought to get used to me like this. Now let me see you.

SYLVIA 2: But suddenly undressing in front of Buddy appealed to me about as much as having my Posture Picture taken at college - where you have to stand stark naked in front of a camera and be marked A, B, C or D depending on how straight you are. Oh some other time?

BUDDY: All right.

SYLVIA 2: And he got dressed again.

SYLVIA 3: I also remember Buddy saying in a sinister way that after I had children I would feel differently: I wouldn't want to write poems any more. So I began to think maybe it was true that when you were

21

married and had children it was like being brain-
washed and afterwards you went about numb as a
slave in a private totalitarian state.

VOICE: 'The Applicant'

SYLVIA 2: First, are you our sort of person?
Do you wear
A glass eye, false teeth or a crutch,
A brace or a hook,
Rubber breasts or a rubber crotch,

Stitches to show something's missing? No,
    no? Then
How can we give you a thing?
Stop crying.
Open your hand.
Empty? Empty. Here is a hand

To fill it and willing
To bring teacups and roll away headaches
And do whatever you tell it.
Will you marry it?
It is guaranteed

To thumb shut your eyes at the end
And dissolve of sorrow.
We make new stock from the salt.
I notice you are stark naked.
How about this suit —

Black and stiff, but not a bad fit
Will you marry it?
It is waterproof, shatterproof, proof
Against fire and bombs through the roof.

22

Believe me, they'll bury you in it.

Now your head, excuse me, is empty.
I have the ticket for that.
Come here, sweetie, out of the closet.
Well, what do you think of that?
Naked as paper to start

But in twenty-five years she'll be silver,
In fifty, gold.
A living doll, everywhere you look.
It can sew, it can cook,
It can talk, talk, talk.

It works, there is nothing wrong with it.
You have a hole, it's a poultice,
You have an eye, it's an image.
My boy, it's your last resort.
Will you marry it, marry it, marry it?

VOICE: She had been subject to fluctuations in mood
    before, but this time, after returning to Wellesley,
    she seemed unable to escape her depression. Every
    act became difficult; eventually the smallest tasks
    seemed almost impossible. She attempted suicide
    with sleeping pills. She was hospitalized, given
    psychiatric treatment and electrical shock therapy.
VOICE: The clinic director says she has been making time
    with Johnny Panic again.
TWO VOICES: Naughty, naughty.
    (The mask appears.)
SYLVIA 3: The white cot is ready. With a terrible gentle-
    ness Miss Milleravage takes the watch from my wrist,

23

the rings from my fingers, the hairpins from my hair. She begins to undress me. When I am bare, I am anointed on the temples and robed in sheets virginal as the first snow. Then, from the four corners of the room and from the door behind me come five false priests in white surgical gowns and masks, whose one life work is to unseat Johnny Panic from his own throne. They extend me full-length on my back on the cot. The crown of wire is placed on my head, the wafer of forgetfulness on my tongue. The masked priests move to their posts and take hold: one of my left leg, one of my right, one of my right arm, one of my left. One behind my head at the metal box where I can't see.

From their cramped niches along the wall, the votaries raise their voices in protest. They begin the devotional chant:

TWO VOICES:

> The only thing to love is Fear itself.
>
> Love of Fear is the beginning of wisdom.
>
> The only thing to love is Fear itself.
>
> May Fear and Fear and Fear be everywhere.

SYLVIA 3: There is no time for Miss Milleravage or the clinic director or the priests to muzzle them.

The signal is given.

At the moment when I think I am lost the face of Johnny Panic appears in a nimbus of arc lights on the ceiling overhead. I am shaken like a leaf in the teeth of glory. His beard is lightning. Lightning is in his eye. His Word charges and illumines the universe. The air crackles with his blue-tongued, lightning-haloed angels. His love is the twenty-storey leap, the rope at the throat, the knife at the heart. He forgets not his own.

SYLVIA 2: I have done it again.

One year in every ten
I manage it —

A sort of walking miracle, my skin
Bright as a Nazi lampshade,
My right foot

A paperweight,
My face a featureless, fine
Jew linen.

Peel off the napkin
O my enemy.
Do I terrify? -

The nose, the eye pits, the full set of teeth?
The sour breath
Will vanish in a day.

Soon, soon the flesh
The grave cave ate will be
At home on me

And I a smiling woman.
I am only thirty.
And like the cat I have nine times to die.

This is Number Three.
What a trash
To annihilate each decade.

What a million filaments.
The peanut-crunching crowd
Shoves in to see

Them unwrap me hand and foot -
The big strip tease.
Gentlemen, ladies

These are my hands,
My knees.
I may be skin and bone,

Nevertheless, I am the same, identical woman
The first time it happened I was ten.
It was an accident.

The second time I meant
To last it out and not come back at all.
I rocked shut

As a seashell.
They had to call and call
And pick the worms off me like sticky pearls.

Dying
Is an art, like everything else.
I do it exceptionally well.

I do it so it feels like hell.
I do it so it feels real.
I guess you could say I've a call.

It's easy enough to do it in a cell
It's easy enough to do it and stay put.
It's the theatrical

Comeback in broad day
To the same place, the same face, the same
   brute
Amused shout:

'A miracle!'
That knocks me out.
There is a charge

For the eyeing of my scars, there is a charge
For the hearing of my heart -
It really goes.

And there is a charge, a very large charge,
For a word or a touch
Or a bit of blood

Or a piece of my hair or my clothes.
So, so, Herr Doktor.
So, Herr Enemy.

I am your opus,
I am your valuable,
The pure gold baby

That melts to a shriek.
I turn and burn.
Do not think I underestimate your great concern.

Ash, ash -
You poke and stir.
Flesh, bone, there is nothing there -

A cake of soap,
A wedding ring,
A gold filling.

Herr God, Herr Lucifer,
Beware
Beware.

Out of the ash
I rise with my red hair
And I eat men like air.   ('Lady Lazarus

VOICE: Midwinter - the doctor and college authorities
    decided she was well enough to leave hospital and
    try college again.

SYLVIA 2: The packed snow cracked underfoot, and
    everywhere I could hear a musical trickle and drip
    as the noon sun thawed icicles and snow crusts that
    would glaze again before nightfall.
    (The mask fades.)
    At college, exams and papers proved I hadn't lost m
    repetitive or my creative intellect, as I had feared.
    My lifelong ambition is to be published in the New
    Yorker.

VOICE: In the June examinations of 1955, Miss S. Plath
    graduated from Smith College 'summa cum laude'.

SYLVIA 2 (excited): And gets a Fulbright to Newnham
    College, Cambridge.

VOICE: At Newnham, she lived in an attic studio room
    decorated with bouquets of bright flowers, piles of
    fresh fruit from the market, and vivid postcard
    reprints of Picasso.

SYLVIA 2: Biking to town and classes at least ten miles
    a day.

SYLVIA 1: Cheering the Royal procession in the rain.

SYLVIA 3: Punting up the River Cam to Grantchester,
    for tea, scones and Cambridgeshire honey.

SYLVIA 2: Arguing politics with students from every
    continent, in the Cafe Expresso houses.

SYLVIA 1: Acting in Jonson's <u>Bartholomew Fair</u> for the
    dramatic society.

SYLVIA 3: Eating bindhi gusht and prawn pelavi at the
    Indian Taj Mahal.

VOICE: In February 1956 she went to a party and met
    Ted Hughes.

ANOTHER VOICE: On June 16th of the same year Sylvia
    Plath and Ted Hughes were married in London, with
    Sylvia's mother as witness. It was Bloomsday.

VOICE: After a summer in France and Spain, they
    returned to Cambridge where they settled in a flat
    overlooking Grantchester Meadows. He started
    teaching English at a secondary modern school. She
    continued her university studies.

ANOTHER VOICE: She was riding weekly on a horse
    called Ariel. Several years later she recalled her
    sensations, when her horse had bolted and she had
    galloped home two miles, free of stirrup or rein.
    (<u>SYLVIA 3 rises.</u>)

SYLVIA 3: Stasis in darkness.
            Then the substanceless blue
            Pour of tor and distances.

            God's lioness,
            How one we grow,
            Pivot of heels and knees! - The furrow

29

Splits and passes, sister to
The brown arc
Of the neck I cannot catch,

Nigger-eye
Berries cast dark
Hooks -

Black sweet blood mouthfuls,
Shadows.
Something else

Hauls me through air -
Thighs, hair;
Flakes from my heels.

White
Godiva, I unpeel -
Dead hands, dead stringencies.

And now I
Foam to wheat, a glitter of seas.
The child's cry

Melts in the wall.
And I
Am the arrow,

The dew that flies
Suicidal, at one with the drive
Into the red

Eye, the cauldron of morning.   ('Ariel')

VOICE: In spring 1957 they moved to the United States . . .

VOICE: . . . Land of the cookie sheet, central heating and frozen orange juice . . .

VOICE: . . . and after a summer on Cape Cod, she accepted her chosen profession and prepared to teach English as an instructor at Smith College.

SYLVIA 3: I'll be scared to death the first day, but am really excited about it: if I had a million-dollar fellowship to write in Italy next year I would refuse it: I've gotten sick of living on great grants and feel very much that need . . . of 'giving out' in some kind of work: my way, apart from writing, I know is teaching. I'll probably learn a hell of a lot more from them than they do from me, but seven years age and reading difference between me and my pupils is enough to give me courage.

VOICE: Years later a senior colleague said:'She was one of the two or three finest instructors ever to appear in the English department at Smith College. Her classroom performance was thrilling. She was an astonishingly good teacher with great warmth and generosity. '

SYLVIA 3: But although I loved teaching the great conflict was with writing. I wore my eyes out on seventy student themes every other week and had no energy for writing a thing. So, we went on a shoestring for a year, in Boston, writing to see what we could do.

VOICE: Interview from Mademoiselle magazine. Miss Plath, what sort of work ambitions do you and your husband share? And what is it like being married to another writer?

SYLVIA 2: Both of us want to write as much as possible, and we do. Ted likes a table he made in a window niche from two planks, and I have a fetish about my grandmother's desk with an ivy and grape design burned into the wood. In the morning we have coffee (a concession to America) and in the afternoon, tea (a concession to England). That's about the extent of our differences. We do criticize each other's work but we write poems that are as distinct and different as our fingerprints themselves must be.

VOICE: In February 1960 they moved to London.

(SYLVIA 3 puts new coloured cover on a book.)

SYLVIA 3 (to audience): I think I am beginning to wither to one of my silent centres.

(Thinks better of it, tries another cover.)

Nothing stinks like a pile of unpublished writing, which remark I guess shows I still don't have a pure motive (O-it's-such-fun-I-just-can't-stop-who-cares if-it's-published-or-read) about writing. - I still want to see it finally ritualized in print.

VOICE: She was repeatedly submitting the manuscript of her book of poems, under different titles.

(She changes cover again.)

SYLVIA 3: I am wondering if I shall ever write a good poem again.

VOICE: Finally in 1960, the book of poems was accepted for publication by Heinemann Ltd., London. It was now entitled

SYLVIA 3 (turning cover to audience): The Colossus!

(She is handed a sheaf of newspaper clippings.) Press cuttings!

(During the following, the others start to assemble equipment as for a home childbirth.)

From The Antioch Review. I like her animals especially the goats and pigs. Playing along even in

the most grotesque of the poems is a babble of un-
abashed humour. She likes life . . . Oh rare response!
The New Statesman, December 1960. The baffling
obliqueness of the work in general and the particular
unruliness of the imagery are worthy faults.
Roy Fuller in the London Magazine. The strongest
impression these poems leave is of cleverness, but
too many poems have no other point than their own
skill. If Miss Plath can let things slip a bit (without
gushing) her next book may remove all one's doubts.
(The cry of a child is heard.)

ONE VOICE:

      What is so real

      As the cry of a child?

      The clear vowels rise like balloons.

SYLVIA 3: I had always imagined myself hitching up on
to my elbows on the delivery table after it was all
over - dead white of course, with no make-up from
the awful ordeal, but smiling and radiant with my
hair down to my waist, and reaching out for my first
little squirmy child, and saying its name whatever
it was.

VOICE: At 5.45 a.m. on April 1st 1960, Frieda Rebecca
was born at home after an unexpectedly short labour.
It was exactly sunrise on the day she regularly
marked as the first day of spring.

SYLVIA 3: The experience was amazing. The intimacy,
privacy, homieness of it all seemed just what I
needed.

VOICE: She was attended by Sister Mardee, a young
Indian midwife.

VOICE: The baby was washed in her largest Pyrex baking
dish.

33

SYLVIA 3: By the afternoon I was eating yoghurt and maple syrup, and typing on my Olivetti.

(SYLVIA 3 types during the following. SYLVIA 2 peels potatoes, SYLVIA 1 feeds baby.)

SYLVIA 1, 2, 3:

> Love set you going like a fat gold watch.
> The midwife slapped your footsoles, and your bald cry
> Took its place among the elements.
>
> Our voices echo, magnifying your arrival.
> New statue
> In a drafty museum, your nakedness
> Shadows our safety. We stand round blankly as walls.
>
> I'm no more your mother
> Than the cloud that distils a mirror to reflect its own slow
> Effacement at the wind's hand.
>
> All night your moth-breath
> Flickers among the flat pink roses. I wake to listen:
> A far sea moves in my ear.

(from 'Morning Song')

(SYLVIA 3 stops typing and pulls paper from typewriter.)

SYLVIA 3: The issues of our time which pre-occupy me at the moment are the genetic effects of fall-out and the terrifying marriage of big business and the military in America. Does this influence the kind of poetry I write? Yes, but in a sidelong fashion. My poems do

34

not turn out to be about Hiroshima, but about a child forming itself finger by finger in the dark. They are not about the terrors of mass extinction, but about the bleakness of the moon over a yew tree in a neighbouring garden.

VOICE: She now had a fellowship on which to work, but the following year was not easy. In rapid succession she had a miscarriage, an appendectomy, and then became pregnant again. But she continued writing.

SYLVIA 3 (typing): 'Tulips'

SYLVIA 1: The tulips are too excitable, it is winter here.
Look how white everything is, how quiet, how
snowed-in.
I am learning peacefulness, lying by myself
quietly
As the light lies on these white walls, this bed,
these hands.
I am nobody; I have nothing to do with explosions.
I have given my name and my day-clothes up
to the nurses
And my history to the anaesthetist and my body
to surgeons . . .

I have let things slip, a thirty-year-old cargo
boat
Stubbornly hanging on to my name and address.
They have swabbed me clear of my loving
associations.
Scared and bare on the green plastic-pillowed
trolley
I watched my teaset, my bureaus of linen, my
books
Sink out of sight, and the water went over my

35

head.

I am a nun now, I have never been so pure . . .

The tulips are too red in the first place, they
    hurt me.
Even through the gift paper I could hear them
    breathe
Lightly, through their white swaddlings, like
    an awful baby.
Their redness talks to my wound, it corres-
    ponds.
They are subtle: they seem to float, though
    they weigh me down,
Upsetting me with their sudden tongues and
    their colour,
A dozen red lead sinkers round my neck.

Nobody watched me before, now I am watched.
The tulips turn to me, and window behind me
Where once a day the light slowly widens and
    slowly thins,
And I see myself, flat, ridiculous, a cut-paper
    shadow
Between the eye of the sun and the eyes of the
    tulips
And I have no face, I have wanted to efface
    myself.
The vivid tulips eat my oxygen . . .

The walls, also, seem to be warming them-
    selves.
The tulips should be behind bars like dangerous
    animals;

They are opening like the mouth of some great
    African cat,
And I am aware of my heart: it opens and
    closes
Its bowl of red blooms out of sheer love of me.
The water I taste is warm and salt, like the
    sea,
And comes from a country far away as health.

(Brief sounds of the sea.)

SYLVIA 3 (whispers): This is the sea, then, this great
    abeyance.

(Sea fades.)

VOICE: In summer 1961 the Hughes family bought a
    peaked, thatched country house in Devon. The house
    was set in an orchard of apple trees and faced a
    twelfth-century Anglican church across an acre of
    green.

SYLVIA 3 (writing in diary): We have an oak at the back,
    a bright yellow door at the front and we face the
    church across an acre of stinging nettles. The front
    gate opens just under the corner of the church grave-
    yard. What I most admire here is the person who
    masters an area of practical experience, and can
    teach me something. I mean, my local midwife has
    taught me how to keep bees. Well, she can't under-
    stand anything I write. And I find myself liking her
    more than most poets.

(SYLVIA 2 appears in Beekeeper's outfit.)

SYLVIA 2: I ordered this, this clean wood box
        Square as a chair and almost too heavy to lift.
        I would say it was the coffin of a midget
        Or a square baby

Were there not such a din in it.

The box is locked, it is dangerous.
I have to live with it overnight
And I can't keep away from it.
There are no windows so I can't see what is i
    there.
There is only a little grid, no exit.

I put my eye to the grid.
It is dark, dark,
With the swarmy feeling of African hands
Minute and shrunk for export,
Black on black, angrily clambering.

How can I let them out?
It is the noise that appals me most of all,
The unintelligible syllables.
It is like a Roman mob,
Small, taken one by one, but my god, togethe

I lend my ear to furious Latin.
I am not a Caesar.
I have simply ordered a box of maniacs.
They can be sent back.
They can die, I need feed them nothing, I am
    the owner.

I wonder how hungry they are .
I wonder if they would forget me
If I just undid the locks and stood back and
    turned into a tree.
There is the laburnum, its blond colonnades,

And the petticoats of the cherry.

They might ignore me immediately
In my moon suit and funeral veil.
I am no source of honey
So why should they turn on me?
Tomorrow I will be sweet God, I will set them
   free.

The box is only temporary.

('The Arrival of the Bee Box')

SYLVIA 3 (returning with diary): How I love the millions
   of birds who live in the thatch, even the blue tits who
   drink the cream off our milk! I think our little local
   church very lovely - it has eight bellringers and some
   fine stained-glass windows, but I must say the
   Anglican religion seems terribly numb and cold and
   grim to me . . . All the awful emphasis on our weak-
   ness and sinfulness and being able to do nothing but
   through Christ . . . But I do want Frieda to have the
   experience of Sunday School, so I may keep up the
   unsatisfactory practice of going, although I disagree
   with almost everything.

VOICE: 'Mothers' - a short story by Sylvia Plath.
   (They pick up books and read/playact the story.)

SYLVIA 3: When Esther came down, Rose was waiting
   just outside the door, smartly dressed for church.

ROSE: At her side stood a blond, bony-faced woman with
   bright blue eyelids and no eyebrows. 'This is Mrs.
   Nolan, the wife of the pubkeeper at The White Hart.
   Mrs. Nolan has never come to the Mother's Union
   Meeting because she hasn't had anyone to go with, so

39

I'm bringing her to this month's meeting together
with you. '

SYLVIA 3: I let us through the seven-foot-high, stockade-
like gate and latched it behind us.

ROSE (offering mints): Polo? Polo? We're meeting in
the church today. We don't always meet in the church
though - only when there's new members joining up.

SYLVIA 3: Are you new in town too?

MRS. NOLAN: I've been here six years.

SYLVIA 3: Why you must know everybody by now!

MRS. NOLAN: Hardly a soul.

SYLVIA 3: If Mrs. Nolan, an Englishwoman by her looks
and accent, and a pubkeeper's wife as well, felt
herself a stranger in Devon after six years, what
hope had I, an American, of infiltrating that rooted
society.

ROSE (to audience): The interior of the church was very
bright. Already the back pews were filling, so we
found an empty pew halfway up the aisle.

(ROSE kneels, SYLVIA and MRS. NOLAN stand.)

MRS. NOLAN: I never come here much.

SYLVIA 3: Neither do I.

(ROSE rises.)

The church filled rapidly now. The Rector's wife,
long-faced, angular, kind, tiptoed from her front pew
pass out copies of the Mother's Union Service Book.
I felt the baby throb and kick, and placidly thought,
I am a mother; I belong here. The Rector stepped
forward and repeated at length an anecdote which had
formed the substance of his last Evensong sermon. T
he brought out an awkward, even embarrassing metap
I had heard him use at a baptism ceremony a week
earlier, about physical and spiritual abortions. Surel

40

the Rector was indulging himself. Rose slipped
another peppermint between her lips, and Mrs.
Nolan wore the glazed, far-off look of an unhappy
seeress. Four o'clock struck before the Rector
allowed us to depart.

MRS. NOLAN: You staying for tea?

SYLVIA 3: That's what I came for. I think we deserve it.

MRS. NOLAN: When's your next baby?

SYLVIA 3: Any minute.

ROSE (to audience): We left the church together with
Brenda the wife of the greengrocer, and stylish Mrs.
Hotchkiss who lived on Widdop Hill and bred Alsatians.
In a few minutes we were in the Church Hall.

SYLVIA 3: There was a startling number of cakes, all
painstakingly decorated, some with cherries and nuts,
and some with sugar lace. Already the Rector had
taken a stand at the head of one table, and his wife at
the head of the other and the townswomen were
crowding into the closely-spaced chairs below. We
sat and settled.

MRS. NOLAN: What do you do here?

SYLVIA 3: Oh, I have the baby. I type some of my
husband's work.

ROSE: Her husband writes for the radio.

MRS. NOLAN: I paint.

SYLVIA 3: What in?

MRS. NOLAN: Oils mainly. But I'm no good.

SYLVIA 3: Ever tried watercolour?

MRS. NOLAN: Oh yes, but you have to be good, you have
to get it right the first time.

SYLVIA 3: What do you paint, then? Portraits?

MRS. NOLAN: Do you suppose we can smoke? We can
smoke can't we?

41

ROSE: Oh, I don't think so, not in the church rooms.

SYLVIA 3: Oh, why? Is it a fire law? Or something
    religious?

    But nobody knew. Then suddenly the swing doors
    flew open to admit a flushed young woman with a
    steaming tray. 'The sausages, the sausages.' I felt
    very hungry, almost faint. Even the ribbons of clear,
    hot grease oozing from my sausage didn't stop me.
    I took a large bite and so did Mrs. Nolan.
    (They both mime it.)

ROSE: At that point the Rector bowed his head and every-
    body said Grace.
    (Prays.)
    Amen. (to SYLVIA 3 and MRS. NOLAN)
    Have some sausages.

    In the general flurry of clapping and smiles, the
    Rector came to sit in an empty chair next to Mrs.
    Nolan.

SYLVIA 3: I listened unashamedly as I ate through my
    plate of buttered dough bread and assorted cakes.
    The Rector made some odd, jocular reference to never
    finding Mrs. Nolan in, at which her clear blonde's
    skin turned a bright shade of pink, then said 'I'm
    sorry, the reason I've not called is because I thought
    you were a divorcée. I usually make it a point not to
    bother them.'

MRS. NOLAN: Oh it doesn't matter. It doesn't matter
    now does it?

SYLVIA 3: The Rector finished with some welcoming
    homily which escaped me so confused and outraged
    was I by Mrs. Nolan's predicament.

MRS. NOLAN: I shouldn't have come. Divorced women
    aren't supposed to come.

42

SYLVIA 3: That's ridiculous. I'm going. Let's go now.

ROSE: I'll go with you. Cecil will want his tea.

SYLVIA 3: At the townhall Mrs. Nolan said Good-bye . . .

MRS. NOLAN: Good-bye . . .

SYLVIA 3: And started off down the hill to her husband's
pub.

The river road faded, at its first dip, in a bank of
wet blue fog; she was lost to view in a few minutes.
(to ROSE) I didn't know they didn't allow divorcées.

ROSE: Oh no, they don't like 'em. Polo? Mrs. Hotchkiss said that even if Mrs. Nolan wanted to join the
Mother's Union, she couldn't.

SYLVIA 3: The gravestones, greenly luminous in the
thick dusk, looked as if their ancient lichens might
possess some magical power of phosphorescence.
We passed under the churchyard with its flat, black
yew, and as the chill of the evening wore through
our coats and the afterglow of tea, Rose crooked out
one arm, and I took it.

(A baby cries. They put down the books.)

VOICE: What is so real as the cry of a child?
The clear vowels rise like balloons.
On January 17th 1962, Nicholas Farrar Hughes was
born with his father and the local midwife in attend-
ance. (The baby in a Moses basket is placed in the
centre of the floor.)

SYLVIA 3: He is a true Hughes - craggy, dark, quiet
and smiley. I write a poem to him: 'Nick and the
Candlestick'.

A mother nurses her baby son by candlelight and
finds in him a beauty which, while it may not ward
off the world's ill does redeem her share of it.

SYLVIA 2.(sitting with the baby, lights a candle.):

43

I am a miner. The light burns blue.
Waxy stalactites
Drip and thicken, tears

The earthen womb
exudes from its dead boredom.
Black bat airs

Wrap me, raggy shawls,
Cold homicides.
They weld to me like plums.

Old cave of calcium
Icicles, old echoer.
Even the newts are white,

Those holy Joes.
And the fish, the fish -
Christ! They are panes of ice,

A vice of knives,
A piranha
Religion, drinking

Its first communion out of my live toes.
The candle
Gulps and resumes its small altitude,

Its yellows hearten.
O love, how did you get here?
O embryo

Remembering, even in sleep,

Your crossed position.
The blood blooms clean

In you, ruby.
The pain
You wake to is not yours.

Love, love,
I have hung our cave with roses.
With soft rugs -

The last of Victoriana.
Let the stars
Plummet to their dark address,

Let the mercuric
Atoms that cripple drip
Into the terrible well,

You are the one
Solid the spaces lean on, envious.
You are the baby in the barn.

VOICE: Summer 1962. The year was proving to be a very
bad and difficult one. Not only her health but her
emotional life too was causing her great disturbances.
Her reactions to things became violent and enraged,
thus a visit to a friend, a young mother like herself,
resulted in this poem, 'Lesbos'.

SYLVIA 3 (peeling potatoes):
Viciousness in the kitchen!
The potatoes hiss.
It is all Hollywood, windowless,

The fluorescent light wincing on and off like
    a terrible migraine,
Coy paper strips for doors -
Stage curtains, a widow's frizz.
And I, love, am a pathological liar,
And my child - look at her, face down on the
    floor,
Little unstrung puppet, kicking to disappear -
Why she is schizophrenic,
Her face red and white, a panic,
You have stuck her kittens outside your windo
In a sort of cement well
Where they crap and puke and cry and she
    can't hear.
You say you can't stand her,
The bastard's a girl.
You who have blown your tubes like a bad
    radio . . .
You say I should drown the kittens. Their
    smell!
You say I should drown my girl.
She'll cut her throat at ten if she's mad at
    two . . .

Meanwhile there's a stink of fat and baby crap
I'm doped and thick from my last sleeping pill
The smog of cooking, the smog of hell
Floats our heads, two venomous opposites,
Our bones, our hair.
I call you Orphan, orphan. You are ill.
The sun gives you ulcers, the wind gives you
    T.B. . . .

Now I am silent, hate

Up to my neck,

Thick, thick . . .

I am packing the hard potatoes like good
   clothes,

I am packing the babies,

I am packing the sick cats.

O vase of acid,

It is love you are full of. You know who you
   hate,

He is hugging his ball and chain down by the
   gate . . .

Your voice my ear-ring,

Flapping and sucking, blood-loving bat.

That is that. That is that.

You peer from the door,

Sad hag

'Every woman's a whore.

I can't communicate.'

VOICE: She decided to take a holiday, and spent some
   time in Ireland. But her attacks of flu and fever
   continued, and then in the middle of 1962 she and her
   husband separated. A few days before Christmas
   she moved to London with Frieda (now two and a half)
   and Nick (eleven months).

SYLVIA 3: A small miracle happened - I'd been to Yeats's
   tower at Ballylea while in Ireland and thought it the
   most beautiful and peaceful place in the world; then,
   walking desolately round my beloved Primrose Hill
   in London and brooding on the hopelessness of ever
   finding a flat . . . I passed Yeats's house: with its
   blue plaque 'Yeats lived here' which I'd often passed
   and longed to live in. (A slide of the plaque is pro-
   jected on to the black gauze.) A signboard was up -

'Flats to rent' - I flew to the agent. By a miracle -
you can only know if you've ever tried to flat-hunt in
London - I was the first to apply . . . I am here on
a five years' lease and it is utter heaven . . . and
it's Yeats's house, which right now means a lot to me
(During the following speech SYLVIA 3 sits with
projector and runs slides of her house in Primrose
Hill - the facade; street sign 'Fitzroy Road' etc.)
SYLVIA 1: A letter to Peter Orr. I'm coming up to
London again this Monday for a couple of days to
make arrangements about my new place. It should
amuse you with your shared mania for Ireland, that
I'll be living in Yeats's house, plaque and all. The
story is quite incredible and a bit witchy. I've
always wanted to live in this particular house because
of the Yeats mania and on the one day I was up in
London, I happened to walk past, happened to see a
signboard out and the builders in and happened to be
the first to apply. When I got home, very cocky, I
said to my nurse 'I'll just open Yeats's plays and
get a message about the house. ' When I opened my
eyes I was pointing to the words 'Get food and wine
and whatever you need to give you strength and
courage and I will get the house ready' from 'The
Unicorn from the Stars'. Well if Willie wants to get
in touch, it is fine by me. I think I'm a heck of a
better sort than Dorothy Wellesley! I'll send you the
new address when I move in so you can deluge me
with Chesterton there, and a book list of Victoriana,
please. I may not be Eminent, but my God, Victorian.
(Slides end. SYLVIA 3 wraps blanket round her and
starts writing.)

VOICE: She had undergone during the period an extraordinary creative explosion. Earlier in her working life she had worked slowly and meticulously with her thesaurus. Now she wrote poems rapidly, urgently, like vital telegrams. She was writing two or three poems a day.

SYLVIA 3: These new poems of mine have one thing in common. They were all written at about four in the morning - that still, blue almost eternal hour before cockcrow, before the baby's cry, before the glassy music of the milkman setting his bottles.

(A baby's cry. SYLVIA 3 moves to the Moses basket.)

VOICE: One cry, and I stumble from bed, cow-heavy
                  and floral
              In my Victorian nightgown.
              Your mouth opens clean as a cat's. The window
                  square

              Whitens and swallows its dull stars. And now
                  you try
              Your handful of notes;
              The clear vowels rise like balloons.

                                    (from 'Morning Song')

ANOTHER VOICE: Christmas was spent alone in the new flat, with the children.

(SYLVIA 3 opens the Moses basket and takes out two coloured balloons with cat and fish faces crayoned on.)

SYLVIA 3: Since Christmas they have lived with us,
              Guileless and clear,
              Oval soul animals,
              Taking up half the space,
              Moving and rubbing on the silk

49

Invisible air drifts,
Giving a shriek and pop
When attacked, then scooting to rest, barely
    trembling.
Yellow cathead, blue fish — —
Such queer moons we live with. . .

VOICE: The winter of 1962 was the worst in England for
    almost 150 years, since 1814. The snow had begun
    a few days before Christmas and went on and on. By
    New Year the country was at a standstill. Trains
    and cars froze to the spot, water froze solid in the
    pipes, and power stations, unable to cope with the
    demand for heat, broke down continually. Two weeks
    later Sylvia Plath's only novel, The Bell Jar, was
    published.

SYLVIA 3 (writing): From the final chapter of The Bell
    Jar: A fresh fall of snow blanketed the asylum
    grounds - not a Christmas sprinkle, but a man-high
    January deluge, the sort that snuffs out schools and
    offices and churches, and leaves. In a week, if I
    passed my interview with the board of doctors, a
    large black car would drive me west and deposit me
    at the wrought-iron gates of my college. My mother's
    face floated to mind, a pale reproachful moon at her
    last visit to the asylum.

MOTHER: We'll take up where we left off Esther. We'll
    act as if all this were a bad dream.

SYLVIA 3: A bad dream.
                To the person in the bell jar, blank and stoppe
                    as a dead baby,
                The world itself is the bad dream.
                A bad dream.

I remembered everything.
Maybe forgetfulness, like a kind snow, would
numb and cover.

VOICE (to audience): The snow continued on into February.
She was still producing poems at an astonishing rate;
by now most of the poems later to be published as
Ariel had been written. One of these: 'Death & Co'.
(The Blake mask re-appears.)
SYLVIA 3 (writing): This poem is about the double or
schizophrenic nature of death - the marmoreal
coldness of Blake's death mask say, hand in glove
with the fearful softness of worms and water. I
imagine these two aspects of death as two men, two
business friends, who have come to call.
SYLVIA 2: Two,
SYLVIA 1: Of course there are two.
SYLVIA 2: It seems perfectly natural now -
The one who never looks up, whose eyes are
lidded
And balled, like Blake's,
SYLVIA 1: Who exhibits
The birthmarks that are his trademark -
The scald scar of water,
SYLVIA 2: The nude
Verdigris of the condor.
I am red meat. His beak

Claps sidewise: I am not his yet.
SYLVIA 1: He tells me how badly I photograph.
He tells me how sweet
The babies look in their hospital
Icebox, a simple

51

Frill at the neck,
Then the flutings of their Ionian
Death-gowns,
Then two little feet.
He does not smile or smoke.

SYLVIA 2: The other does that,
His hair long and plausive.
Bastard
Masturbating a glitter,
He wants to be loved.

SYLVIA 3: I do not stir.
The frost makes a flower,
The dew makes a star,
The dead bell,
The dead bell.

Somebody's done for.

VOICE: The weather continued monstrous. Meanwhile a
recurrent trouble - her sinuses were bad; the pipes
in her newly converted flat froze solid; there was
still no telephone and no word from the psycho-
therapist.

ANOTHER VOICE: An employment agency had found her
an au pair girl to help with the children and house-
work while Sylvia got on with her writing. The girl -
an Australian - was due to arrive at nine o'clock on
the morning of Monday 11th February.

VOICE: But illness, loneliness, depression and cold,
combined with the demands of two small children,
were too much for her. So when the weekend came

she went off with the babies to stay with friends in another part of London.

The plan was that she would leave early enough on Monday morning to be back in time to welcome the Australian girl. Instead, she decided to go back on the Sunday. The friends were against it, but she was insistent, made a great show of her old competence, and seemed more cheerful than she had done for some time, so they let her go.

About eleven o'clock that night she knocked on the door of the elderly painter who lived below her, asking to borrow some stamps. But she lingered in the doorway, drawing out the conversation until he told her that he got up well before nine in the morning. Then she said good-night and went back upstairs.

The Australian girl arrived punctually at 9 a.m. She rang and knocked a long time but could get no answer. So she went off to search for a telephone kiosk, in order to phone the agency and make sure she had the right address. Sylvia's name was not on either of the doorbells. The girl returned and tried again, still without success. Again she went off to telephone the agency and ask what to do; they told her to go back.

It was now about eleven o'clock. This time she was lucky: some builders had arrived to work in the frozen-up house, and they let her in. When she knocked on Sylvia's door there was no answer and the smell of gas was overpowering. The builders forced the lock and found Sylvia sprawled in the kitchen. She was still warm. She had left a note saying 'Please call the doctor' and giving his telephone number. But it was too late.

53

The coroner's inquest was held four days later on
the 15th and the verdict returned was 'While suffering
from depression she did kill herself.'
SYLVIA 3: The woman is perfected.
Her dead

Body wears the smile of accomplishment,
The illusion of a Greek necessity

Flows in the scrolls of her toga,
Her bare

Feet seem to be saying:
We have come so far, it is over.

Each dead child coiled, a white serpent,
One at each little

Pitcher of milk, now empty.
She has folded

Them back into her body as petals
Of a rose close when the garden

Stiffens and odours bleed
From the sweet, deep throats of the night
        flower.

The moon has nothing to be sad about,
Staring from her hood of bone.

She is used to this sort of thing.
Her blacks crackle and drag.   ('Edge')

THREE WOMEN
A Poem for Three Voices

SETTING: A Maternity Ward and round about

FIRST VOICE:

> I am slow as the world. I am very patient,
> Turning through my time, the suns and stars
> Regarding me with attention.
> The moon's concern is more personal:
> She passes and repasses, luminous as a nurse.
> Is she sorry for what will happen? I do not think so.
> She is simply astonished at fertility.

> When I walk out, I am a great event.
> I do not have to think, or even rehearse.
> What happens in me will happen without attention.
> The pheasant stands on the hill;
> He is arranging his brown feathers.
> I cannot help smiling at what it is I know.
> Leaves and petals attend me. I am ready.

SECOND VOICE:

> When I first saw it, the small red seep, I did not
> > believe it.
> I watched the men walk about me in the office. They
> > were so flat!

There was something about them like cardboard, and
    now I had caught it,
That flat, flat, flatness from which ideas, destruction
Bulldozers, guillotines, white chambers of shrieks
    proceed,
Endlessly proceed - and the cold angels, the abstr-
    actions.
I sat at my desk in my stockings, my high heels,

And the man I work for laughed: 'Have you seen some-
    thing awful?
You are so white, suddenly.' And I said nothing.
I saw death in the bare trees, a deprivation.
I could not believe it. Is it so difficult
For the spirit to conceive a face, a mouth?
The letters proceed from these black keys, and these
    black keys proceed
From my alphabetical fingers, ordering parts,

Parts, bits, cogs, the shining multiples.
I am dying as I sit. I lose a dimension.
Trains roar in my ears, departures, departures!
The silver track of time empties into the distance,
The white sky empties of its promise, like a cup.
These are my feet, these mechanical echoes.
Tap, tap, tap, steel pegs. I am found wanting.

This is a disease I carry home, this is a death.
Again, this is a death. Is it the air,
The particles of destruction I suck up? Am I a pulse
That wanes and wanes, facing the cold angel?
Is this my lover then? This death, this death?
As a child I loved a lichen-bitten name.

Is this the one sin then, this old dead love of death?

THIRD VOICE:

    I remember the minute when I knew for sure.
    The willows were chilling,
    The face in the pool was beautiful, but not mine -
    It had a consequential look, like everything else,
    And all I could see was dangers: doves and words
    Stars and showers of gold - conceptions, conceptions!
    I remember a white, cold wing

    And the great swan, with his terrible look,
    Coming at me, like a castle, from the top of the river.
    There is a snake in swans.
    He glided by; his eye had a black meaning.
    I saw the world in it - small, mean and black,
    Every little word hooked to every little word, and
        act to act.
    A hot blue day had budded into something.

    I wasn't ready. The white clouds rearing
    Aside were dragging me in four directions.
    I wasn't ready.
    I had no reverence.
    I thought I could deny the consequence -
    But it was too late for that. It was too late, and the
        face
    Went on shaping itself with love, as if I was ready.

SECOND VOICE:

    It is a world of snow now. I am not at home.
    How white these sheets are. The faces have no
        features.

They are bald and impossible, like the faces of my
    children,
Those little sick ones that elude my arms.
Other children do not touch me: they are terrible.
They have too many colours, too much life. They
    are not quiet,
Quiet like the little emptinesses I carry.

I have had my chances. I have tried and tried.
I have stitched life into me like a rare organ,
And walked carefully, precariously, like something
    rare.
I have tried not to think too hard. I have tried to be
    natural.
I have tried to be blind in love, like other women,
Blind in my bed, with my dear blind sweet one,
Not looking, through the thick dark, for the face of
    another.

I did not look. But still the face was there,
The face of the unborn one that loved its perfections,
The face of the dead one that could only be perfect
In its easy peace, could only keep holy so.
And then there were other faces. The faces of nations,
Governments, parliaments, societies,
The faceless faces of important men.

It is these men I mind:
They are so jealous of anything that is not flat! They
    are jealous gods
That would have the whole world flat because they are.
I see the Father conversing with the Son.
Such flatness cannot but be holy.

'Let us make a heaven,' they say.
'Let us flatten and launder the grossness from these
   souls.'

FIRST VOICE:

   I am calm. I am calm. It is the calm before some-
      thing awful:
   The yellow minute before the wind walks, when the
      leaves
   Turn up their hands, their pallors. It is so quiet here.
   The sheets, the faces, are white and stopped, like
      clocks.
   Voices stand back and flatten. Their visible hiero-
      glyphs
   Flatten to parchment screens to keep the wind off.
   They paint such secrets in Arabic, Chinese!

   I am dumb and brown. I am a seed about to break.
   The brownness is my dead self, and it is sullen:
   It does not wish to be more, or different.
   Dusk hoods me in blue now, like a Mary.
   O colour of distance and forgetfulness! -
   When will it be, the second when Time breaks
   And eternity engulfs it, and I drown utterly?

   I talk to myself, myself only, set apart -
   Swabbed and lurid with disinfectants, sacrificial.
   Waiting lies heavy on my lids. It lies like sleep,
   Like a big sea. Far off, far off, I feel the first wave
      tug
   Its cargo of agony towards me, inescapable, tidal.
   And I, a shell, echoing on this white beach
   Face the voices that overwhelm, the terrible element.

59

THIRD VOICE:

I am a mountain now, among mountainy women.
The doctors move among us as if our bigness
Frightened the mind. They smile like fools.
They are to blame for what I am, and they know it.
They hug their flatness like a kind of health.
And what if they found themselves surprised, as I
    did?
They would go mad with it.

And what if two lives leaked between my thighs?
I have seen the white clean chamber with its instru-
    ments.
It is a place of shrieks. It is not happy.
'This is where you will come when you are ready. '
The night lights are flat red moons. They are dull
    with blood.
I am not ready for anything to happen.
I should have murdered this, that murders me.

FIRST VOICE:

There is no miracle more cruel than this.
I am dragged by the horses, the iron hooves.
I last. I last it out. I accomplish a work.
Dark tunnel, through which hurtle the visitations,
The visitations, the manifestations, the startled
    faces.
I am the centre of an atrocity.
What pains, what sorrows must I be mothering?

Can such innocence kill and kill? It milks my life.
The trees wither in the street. The rain is corrosive.
I taste it on my tongue, and the workable horrors,

The horrors that stand and idle, the slighted god-
    mothers
With their hearts that tick and tick, with their satchels
    of instruments.
I shall be a wall and a roof, protecting.
I shall be a sky and a hill of good: O let me be!

A power is growing on me, an old tenacity.
I am breaking apart like the world. There is this
    blackness,
This ram of blackness. I fold my hands on a mountain.
The air is thick. It is thick with this working.
I am used. I am drummed into use.
My eyes are squeezed by this blackness.
I see nothing.

SECOND VOICE:

I am accused. I dream of massacres.
I am a garden of black and red agonies. I drink them,
Hating myself, hating and fearing. And now the world
    conceives
Its end and runs toward it, arms held out in love.
It is a love of death that sickens everything.
A dead sun stains the newsprint. It is red.
I lose life after life. The dark earth drinks them.

She is the vampire of us all. So she supports us,
Fattens us, is kind. Her mouth is red.
I know her. I know her intimately -
Old winter-face, old barren one, old time bomb.
Men have used her meanly. She will eat them.
Eat them, eat them, eat them in the end.
The sun is down. I die. I make a death.

61

FIRST VOICE:

Who is he, this blue, furious boy,
Shiny and strange, as if he had hurtled from a star?
He is looking so angrily!
He flew into the room, a shriek at his heel.
The blue colour pales. He is human after all.
A red lotus opens in its bowl of blood;
They are stitching me up with silk, as if I were a
  material.

What did my fingers do before they held him?
What did my heart do with its love?
I have never seen a thing so clear.
His lids are like the lilac-flower
And soft as a moth, his breath.
I shall not let go.
There is no guile or warp in him. May he keep so.

SECOND VOICE:

There is the moon in the high window. It is over.
How winter fills my soul! And that chalk light
Laying its scales on the windows, the windows of
  empty offices,
Empty schoolrooms, empty churches. O so much
  emptiness!
There is this cessation. This terrible cessation of
  everything.
These bodies mounded around me now, these polar
  sleepers -
What blue, moony ray ices their dreams?

I feel it enter me, cold, alien, like an instrument.
And that mad, hard face at the end of it, that O-mouth

Open in its gape of perpetual grieving.
It is she that drags the blood-black sea around
Month after month, with its voices of failure.
I am helpless as the sea at the end of her string.
I am restless. Restless and useless. I, too, create
   corpses.

I shall move north. I shall move into a long blackness.
I see myself as a shadow, neither man nor woman,
Neither a woman, happy to be like a man, nor a man
Blunt and flat enough to feel no lack. I feel a lack.
I hold my fingers up, ten white pickets.
See, the darkness is leaking from the cracks.
I cannot contain it. I cannot contain my life.

I shall be a heroine of the peripheral.
I shall not be accused by isolate buttons,
Holes in the heels of socks, the white mute faces
Of unanswered letters, coffined in a letter case.
I shall not be accused, I shall not be accused.
The clock shall not find me wanting, nor these stars
That rivet in place abyss after abyss.

THIRD VOICE:
I see her in my sleep, my red, terrible girl.
She is crying through the glass that separates us.
She is crying, and she is furious.
Her cries are hooks that catch and grate like cats.
It is by these hooks she climbs to my notice.
She is crying at the dark, or at the stars
That at such a distance from us shine and whirl.

I think her little head is carved in wood,

A red, hard wood, eyes shut and mouth wide open.
And from the open mouth issue sharp cries
Scratching at my sleep like arrows,
Scratching at my sleep, and entering my side.
My daughter has no teeth. Her mouth is wide.
It utters such dark sounds it cannot be good.

FIRST VOICE:

What is it that flings these innocent souls at us?
Look, they are so exhausted, they are all flat out
In their canvas-sided cots, names tied to their wrists,
The little silver trophies they've come so far for.
There are some with thick black hair, there are some
    bald.
Their skin tints are pink or sallow, brown or red;
They are beginning to remember their differences.

I think they are made of water; they have no expression
Their features are sleeping, like light on quiet water.
They are the real monks and nuns in their identical
    garments.
I see them showering like stars on to the world -
On India, Africa, America, these miraculous ones,
These pure, small images. They smell of milk.
Their footsoles are untouched. They are walkers of
    air.

Can nothingness be so prodigal?
Here is my son.
His wide eye is that general, flat blue.
He is turning to me like a little, blind, bright plant.
One cry. It is the hook I hang on.
And I am a river of milk.

I am a warm hill.

SECOND VOICE:

I am not ugly. I am even beautiful.
The mirror gives back a woman without deformity.
The nurses give back my clothes, and an identity.
It is usual, they say, for such a thing to happen.
It is usual in my life, and the lives of others.
I am one in five, something like that. I am not hope-
    less.
I am beautiful as a statistic. Here is my lipstick.

I draw on the old mouth.
The red mouth I put by with my identity
A day ago, two days, three days ago. It was a Friday.
I do not even need a holiday; I can go to work today.
I can love my husband, who will understand.
Who will love me through the blur of my deformity
As if I had lost an eye, a leg, a tongue.

And so I stand, a little sightless. So I walk
Away on wheels, instead of legs, they serve as well.
And learn to speak with fingers, not a tongue.
The body is resourceful.
The body of a starfish can grow back its arms
And newts are prodigal in legs. And may I be
As prodigal in what lacks me.

THIRD VOICE:

She is a small island, asleep and peaceful,
And I am a white ship hooting: Goodbye, goodbye.
The day is blazing. It is very mournful.
The flowers in this room are red and tropical.

They have lived behind glass all their lives, they
    have been cared for tenderly.
Now they face a winter of white sheets, white faces.
There is very little to go into my suitcase.

There are the clothes of a fat woman I do not know.
There is my comb and brush. There is an emptiness.
I am so vulnerable suddenly.
I am a wound walking out of hospital.
I am a wound that they are letting go.
I leave my health behind. I leave someone
Who would adhere to me: I undo her fingers like
    bandages: I go.

SECOND VOICE:

    I am myself again. There are no loose ends.
    I am bled white as wax, I have no attachments.
    I am flat and virginal, which means nothing has
        happened,
    Nothing that cannot be erased, ripped up and scrapped
        begun again.
    These little black twigs do not think to bud,
    Nor do these dry, dry gutters dream of rain.
    This woman who meets me in windows - she is neat.

    So neat she is transparent, like a spirit.
    How shyly she superimposes her neat self
    On the inferno of African oranges, the heel-hung
        pigs.
    She is deferring to reality.
    It is I. It is I -
    Tasting the bitterness between my teeth.
    The incalculable malice of the everyday.

FIRST VOICE:

How long can I be a wall, keeping the wind off?
How long can I be
Gentling the sun with the shade of my hand,
Intercepting the blue bolts of a cold moon?
The voices of loneliness, the voices of sorrow
Lap at my back ineluctably.
How shall it soften them, this little lullaby?

How long can I be a wall around my green property?
How long can my hands
Be a bandage to his hurt, and my words
Bright birds in the sky, consoling, consoling?
It is a terrible thing
To be so open: it is as if my heart
Put on a face and walked into the world.

THIRD VOICE:

Today the colleges are drunk with spring.
My black gown is a little funeral:
It shows I am serious.
The books I carry wedge into my side.
I had an old wound once, but it is healing.
I had a dream of an island, red with cries.
It was a dream, and did not mean a thing.

FIRST VOICE:

Dawn flowers in the great elm outside the house.
The swifts are back. They are shrieking like paper
    rockets.
I hear the sound of the hours
Widen and die in the hedgerows. I hear the moo of
    cows.

The colours replenish themselves, and the wet
Thatch smokes in the sun.
The narcissi open white faces in the orchard.

I am reassured. I am reassured.
These are the clear bright colours of the nursery,
The talking ducks, the happy lambs.
I am simple again. I believe in miracles.
I do not believe in those terrible children
Who injure my sleep with their white eyes, their
    fingerless hands.
They are not mine. They do not belong to me.

I shall meditate upon normality.
I shall meditate upon my little son.
He does not walk. He does not speak a word.
He is still swaddled in white bands.
But he is pink and perfect. He smiles so frequently.
I have papered his room with big roses,
I have painted little hearts on everything.

I do not will him to be exceptional.
It is the exception that interests the devil.
It is the exception that climbs the sorrowful hill
Or sits in the desert and hurts his mother's heart.
I will him to be common,
To love me as I love him,
And to marry what he wants and where he will.

THIRD VOICE:
Hot noon in the meadows. The buttercups
Swelter and melt, and the lovers
Pass by, pass by.

They are black and flat as shadows.
It is so beautiful to have no attachments!
I am solitary as grass. What is it I miss?
Shall I ever find it, whatever it is?

The swans are gone. Still the river
Remembers how white they were.
It strives after them with its lights.
It finds their shapes in a cloud.
What is that bird that cries
With such sorrow in its voice?
I am young as ever, it says. What is it I miss?

SECOND VOICE:
I am at home in the lamplight. The evenings are
    lengthening.
I am mending a silk slip: my husband is reading.
How beautifully the light includes these things.
There is a kind of smoke in the spring air,
A smoke that takes the parks, the little statues
With pinkness, as if a tenderness awoke,
A tenderness that did not tire, something healing.

I wait and ache. I think I have been healing.
There is a great deal else to do. My hands
Can stitch lace neatly on to this material. My husband
Can turn and turn the pages of a book.
And so we are at home together, after hours.
It is only time that weighs upon our hands.
It is only time, and that is not material.

The streets may turn to paper suddenly, but I recover
From the long fall, and find myself in bed,

Safe on the mattress, hands braced, as for a fall.
I find myself again. I am no shadow
Though there is a shadow starting from my feet. I am
    a wife.
The city waits and aches. The little grasses
Crack through stone, and they are green with life.